CONDENSED TALES
OF
SUSPENSE AND HORROR

CONDENSED TALES OF SUSPENSE AND HORROR

Written by:
Angela A. Taylor

With a Foreword by Raye Nelson

Trafford Publishing
Bloomington, Indiana

Order this book online at www.trafford.com
or email orders@trafford.com

Most Trafford titles are also available at major online book retailers.

Printed in Victoria, BC, Canada.

ISBN: 978-1-4269-2447-7 (sc)

Our mission is to efficiently provide the world's finest, most comprehensive book publishing service, enabling every author to experience success. To find out how to publish your book, your way, and have it available worldwide, visit us online at www.trafford.com

Trafford rev. 12/07/2009

www.trafford.com

North America & international
toll-free: 1 888 232 4444 (USA & Canada)
phone: 250 383 6864 • fax: 812 355 4082

DEDICATION

To my mom, brother, sister and Gary

As well as my group home staff
Who have encouraged me all these years!!

FOREWORD

This is a book of great creativity, well thought out and written from the heart. You will laugh and be put in suspense at the same time. Life is full of challenges, but don't let anyone try to hold you back, that is what the author did and is very proud of what she has become.

PREFACE

I wrote these stories because I have always been told to express my creativeness. I thank my bosses who have helped me pay for my computer and given me a chance to put these stories down into print. I also want to thank all the people who have let me use their name in my stories.

TABLE OF CONTENTS

CAMERA

You wouldn't think that a camera would be a killer. At least that is what I thought. My friend Melissa and I came across the killer Polaroid camera. We were going through my biological mother's belongings when we found the camera. My real mother had given me up for adoption when I was just a baby because she was only thirteen. Unfortunately she died in childbirth so I never will get to meet her. Her name was Beth Anne Johann and a thirty one year old man who thought that she was seventeen had impregnated her. I guess she looked old for her age so my father, Cassidy Cocoa, dated her for two months and then dumped her when he found out she was pregnant with me. Apparently he didn't think I was his child. So he turned his back on my mother when she was in the most need of help. I had never met the man. When my friend and I found the camera we took her picture with it and what came out in the developed picture was totally different than what pose Melissa had taken. In the picture she was laying on the floor in my foster parents kitchen, dead as a doornail. We set the camera off to the side because we thought that it was broken. But later that night when we were eating supper Melissa choked to death on her Frito chili cheese pie. She had swallowed a chip whole and was dead within seconds. As I looked down on her I gasped because I remembered the picture and what it showed. My mother, Dani, called 911 but it was to no avail. The paramedics were unable to revive her. After the police and paramedics had left I went to the attic and retrieved the camera and took it to my room to look at it closer. It looked like any other camera. I decided to give it another try. I decided to take a picture of mom and dad and if they died then if they died I would destroy the camera. My dad, Keith, was walking to my parent's bedroom to get ready for bed when I asked him if I could take a picture of him and mom. He sighed heavily but agreed to. I followed him into their bedroom and quickly took mom and dad's picture. I rushed back to my room where I anxiously waited for the picture to develop. Once the picture was completely done developing I saw my parent's car totaled with a light post on top of it. I was in such shock of the detail of the picture that when I went to sit on my bed that I missed it. I don't know how long that I sat there but when I finally tore my eyes away from the photo I had decided not to tell or show anybody the camera. I hid the photo and the camera from my mom because she always looked around my room when she cleaned it. I then went to bed and had a restless night of sleep. I went to school as usual the next day but was called to the principal's office. Before I got there I knew what was coming my way. The principal sat down next to me and told me that my parent's were killed instantly in a crash when there was a car coming at them. They swerved and hit a light post dying on impact. Even though I knew what was coming I broke down and started to cry. I had hoped that it was a coincidence that the camera had predicted Melissa's death. Since I had no other family, even with my adopted parents, I was sent to a different foster house after I gathered the few belongings that I could bring with me. The first thing that I did grab was the camera. On the ride back to the house of my now old foster parent's house I decided to use the camera to kill the people that had hurt me. The officer that had brought me made me rush to get all of my stuff together. I myself wanted to take my time and take in my surroundings for the last time. As we were pulling away I said a silent prayer for Keith and Dani Comstich since it was part my fault that they died. I also said a silent prayer for Melissa Moocher. As we pulled up to a trailer house a woman came out and opened the passenger side door. "Hello, my name is Tina Turbo. My husband, Brad, is at work right now so you wont be able to meet him right now." I nodded and said, "I'm Lark." I didn't know what to say what my last name was since the people that I knew were dead. Tina seemed to understand that I needed a hug. She embraced me and I held on for a few seconds longer than I should have but I needed it. I felt like everyone had deserted me. But I also knew that it was part my fault. After I brought my few belongings in I met Tina and Brad's son, Larry. He was a year older than me and didn't seem too happy to welcome me into his house. But he put a strained smile on his face and shook my hand. As the next few days passed I started to get accustomed to my new surroundings. I still went to the same school but I had to catch the bus at six in the morning. It was my decision to continue going to the same school so I could kill the bullies that teased Melissa and me when she and I were going to school together. The two people that had decided to go after were Sara Summer and Lisa Lover. They were what you would call the schoolyard bullies that never grew up. They were also fourteen but always acted older and tougher than a fourteen year old. I approached them one Friday with my camera and asked them if I could take a picture of them. They said that I could if they could break my nose. I eagerly agreed and took their picture. I was tempted to run after I took it but I stood still as they both punched me in the nose. Both managed to break my nose but it was worth it. I ran to the bathroom and waited with bated breath. When the picture was finally developed I was surprised to see myself standing over the two of them with their heads all bashed up. There was blood on the ground and the wall behind them that I recognized as the schoolyard. I was confused and happy at the same time but what I didn't know was that they would die that very same day. I was waiting for the school bus when Sara and Lisa came running at me ready to tackle me. If someone hadn't yelled at me to watch out they would have ran into me. Instead I swerved out of the way and they ran head first into the wall that was behind me. As I looked down at their lifeless body, I grinned. It had worked perfectly. They were dead and all that I had suffered was a broken nose. I later heard that they weren't happy with only giving me a broken nose. They wanted me dead just like Melissa. Unfortunately another student told the principal that I had taken their photo and what the picture showed because apparently I had dropped the picture. The person that found it and turned it in was A.J. Arsenic. He thought it was strange that four hours before they were dead that I had a photograph of the accident. I was forced to turn the camera in to the principal. But for some strange reason when Mr. Pajari took my picture it showed me exactly as I was in his office. Since he was unable to prove that it was a planned act to kill them he was forced to let me go. I sat in silence the whole way home not even listening to Tina and Brad talk to me. I was too busy examining the camera. Why had it taken my picture correctly? Was I going to die? After we got to the Turbo house we talked about my future and where I wanted to go with it. I decided to meet my father. Even if it would be against my real mom's wishes I needed to meet him and ask him if he knew about this camera. Brad and Tina agreed to contact my social worker and ask her if I could meet him. It took two long weeks before they were able to track down my biological mother's grave and after I visited it I was an emotional wreck but it made me even more determined to find my dad. I jumped from foster home to foster home for three months as we got closer and closer to Cassidy. I moved from town to town where he had lived for the past fifteen years. He had moved around a lot but we eventually found him and he agreed to meet him if I took a DNA test. When it came back positively he agreed to meet me even if it was unwillingly. But when he saw me he said that it brought back memories of my mother. We talked for hours and hours although I chose to wait to ask him about the camera. We decided to meet again the very next day at which I would bring up the topic of the camera. I showed it to him and when he saw it he inhaled sharply and asked in a hushed voice where I had gotten it. I explained to him what had happened for the past four months. He said that the real reason why Beth had died was because the two of them had invented the camera together and when he took her picture it predicted her death. It was suppose to only predict it not actually come true. It turns out that she didn't die in childbirth but from the camera. As an apology Cassidy agreed to now take me in and raise me as his daughter. Together we came to the conclusion that we would destroy the camera. The death from it is now over with. But I will still always say a prayer for Melissa Moocher and Keith and Dani Comstich. May they rest in peace forever.

CLOUDS

Clouds. They seem harmless enough, but not to me. They are dangerous and can kill you. Let me explain to you why I think this way. It all started out on a cloudy day where I was running late to my CPR class. I don't really remember what happened that day, but my mother told me all about it. I was walking out to my car and she was driving by. Just as she turned the corner at the end of the block when there was a crash of thunder pulsating through my body. It was at that moment that I came to be possessed with the seed of Satan. That was the last thing I felt for a week. Then instead of going to class I went to a bar that was open all day. It was there that I met Larry Paper. He was the leader of the gang The Scissors. We got to talking, as we consumed beer after beer. It turns out that he too was possessed but his possession was with an imp or small demon. That meant that he was to follow my orders. The only reason that he was not possessed with Satan's seed was because he was an experiment. He was used to see if he could remain on earth without attracting too much attention. Since he succeeded I was chosen to be the next one to be possessed. Larry and I came up with the plan to go to the fair in town on Saturday and collect people to join us in our crusade to destroy the world. We would gather a group of ten people and bring them to an abandoned warehouse, once there we would channel some of our power into them from us. So that Saturday we put our plan into action. We gathered Beth Johns, Dani Veal, Britt Willy, Kady Mayflower, Luke Sky, Brad and Hannah Grunt, Ashley Jerky, Garret Ferret and Jim Western. Unfortunately that was the only part of our plan that went right. Somehow the cops found out and we were interrupted in the middle of the power exchange. Since Larry was only an imp he was unable to disappear into thin air like I was able to. He was later hung for murdering Kearsty Kilts. I was found four days later, six days after my possession started, by my family while walking down the street. They tried convincing me into getting into their car. When I wouldn't get in I used my powers to make their car explode because they were trying to take me away. I regret it now but it is too late to take any of the bad things that I did to my family and friends. May my siblings Heather, Ted, Tina, Jackie and Keith and parents Katie and Brandon rest in peace. My friend was the only one that didn't die in the car explosion.

Jona escaped with a few burns. Once she was released from the hospital later that day she went straight to a psychic to see why I was so unwilling to go with my family. The psychic, Lark Lunch was able to tell her that I was being possessed by the devil. At first Jona didn't believe her but eventually she faced facts and asked Lark what she was suppose to do. Lark told her that she had less than twelve hours to find me and get me to drink a potion that she concocted. If she didn't drink it in time then she would lose me. I would explode into a million little pieces. So Lark teamed up with Jona and went back to the bar where I had met Larry. Lucky for them I was there looking for my next partner in crime. By the time that they got there they had five hours left. Jona came up with the idea of her going in and slipping the concoction into my beer. Fortunately for me I had the power to see into the future so after Jona poured it into my beer I used my powers to make her sneeze. I quickly switched our beers and when she drank it she started foaming at the mouth. Within moments Lark was dead. I then simply got up and went to leave. But it was Jona waiting outside that put a kink in my plan. She grabbed me by my shoulders and shook me for some reason this brought me back to reality. I looked around confused and wondering how I got to that bar. All Jona could do was hug me and cry. Suddenly she gasped and let me go. She quickly asked if I had drunk my beer. Of course I didn't know what she was talking about. She started crying and rushed into the bar. She quickly returned crying even harder than I had ever seen her cry. Jona then led me to her car saying she would explain everything to me on the way to Lark's house to find another bottle of the concoction. But as we searched her house I suddenly I started to swell up. Just as Jona looked up I exploded. But I didn't leave the house. Instead I floated up near the ceiling. I said Jona and she looked around very confused. Once she looked up she almost fainted away in shock. We decided then that we wouldn't let my death stop us from helping others in my condition. Thankfully we were able to find a book in Lark's house that told us how to make the concoction that I was suppose to drink. It is now the year 2127 and Jona's great granddaughter, Lori, has taken over for Jona. We have saved over a dozen people from being exploded, but unfortunately we were unable to save all of the victims. We only lost three souls and those souls have now joined us in the hunt to save people. Shawn watches over the east coast, Leslie watches over the west coast and Cara watches over the southern states. What makes it easier is the fact that we noticed that only females have been the victim. We find this strange but it does help us a lot. Mainly because in the past twenty years there have been a large decrease in the number of females born in the world. And another thing that we all find strange is the fact that there has been no news that there have been people exploding without any reason in other countries. But Lori and I send people that were possessed but lived to other countries to keep an eye on the countries in the whole world. But then in the year 2201 Lori died without having children. That meant that I was all alone in my hunt to find possessed people in the northern states. That was when it all started going bad. Satan knew that there was nobody helping me stop him from attacking the northern states. So when we had an outbreak of possessions mainly in Minnesota. That was when I deserted my post for one day as I went to other countries to try and find someone, anyone, to try and help me stop Satan from killing anyone else. I got lucky when I arrived in England and met Adam Metserton. He had come up with a vaccination that can prevent you from being possessed. The only reason that he didn't tell any others or me in our group was because he only had one person volunteered to take it. Most women were afraid to get a shot for something that they didn't believe in. so what we decided to do was convince doctors to insist that all female babies be vaccinated at birth to prevent the result that I ended up with. Thankfully we found two twin doctors named Cassidy and Ryan Basswood. They had a sister named Lisa that died because of being possessed by an imp. That was news to us because we thought that it was the seed of Satan that was affecting all of these poor souls. We got together and with the twin's help we were able to come up with a law worldwide that required all girls to have this vaccination at birth. All I can say is thank you Ryan and Cassidy Basswood. You saved a number of women's lives.

CURSES

I have a curse but it isn't like any other curse you have heard of like a gypsy or voodoo curse. In a way I have three curses. I am a vampire, werewolf and zombie. I don't recall how I got this way or if there are others out there like me. But I am determined to find out how I got this curse. My life is the most challenging life you will ever find. But I do wish that there were somebody out there that has the same curses. Or even one curse would be nice. I just want somebody that I can relate to with my problems. Lucky enough for me I found somebody that can help. Her name is Britt Brat and she is a scientist who can travel back in time in a machine that she built. It would be a challenge but we would find out my past even if it killed us. To start with she taught me how to control my transformations. Thankfully I knew when each transformation would occur. On the first week of the month I would be a zombie, the second week I would be a vampire, the third week I would be a werewolf and in the final week of the month I would be human. We decided to start out in the fourth week of June because I could control my human stage more than any other stage. The first clue that we decided to investigate was a birth announcement from 1988 in an old newspaper that looked like me when Britt did her age comparison on her computer. The paper said that I was born September 25, my full name is Kady Sally Olsen, and my parents were Beth Anne and Pete Olsen. We also found out I have seven siblings. Their names were Kearsty, Larry, Keith, Sabrina, Dani, Ashley and Lori. I arrived at Britt's house at six on Monday morning to go back in time thirty-three years. Back to the time that I was born to see if we can find my family. Hopefully they could shed some light on my life and how I got these curses. After we had our plans finalized we climbed onto her time machine pad and Britt punched in the date 9/26/1988 on the keypad beside the transport pad. All of a sudden we felt a jerk upward and the next thing that I realize we were standing outside a building sign that said Heather Welcome Hospital. It was the hospital that I was supposed to be born in. We hid the transport pad in a bush by the sign and headed inside the hospital. We asked the nurse at the desk where we could find a Beth Anne Olsen. She told us the room number and the floor number and we headed straight there. As we headed to the room we decided to tell her that we were friends of her husband, my father, and ask to see the new baby. But when we got there we heard her crying and a man was trying to comfort her. We knocked on the door and entered the room. When I first saw my parents I was speechless. Thankfully Britt came up with the story that we were walking past the room to see a friends baby when we heard her crying and was wondering if there was anything that we could do to help out. Mom started crying even harder and dad said that they just lost their baby. Britt and I looked at each other confused. How was it possible that they had lost their baby when I was standing there before them? It was confusing to me as to how this was possible. We apologized and went back out to the transport pad. We stood there trying to figure it out. We decided to go even farther back in time and arrive at the hospital on the day that I was born and pretend to be volunteer nurses and be there the exact time that I was born. So we went back in time one day. We dressed as nurses and went into the room that my parents were in the day before. We got lucky because they had just arrived at the hospital shortly before we did. It was weird to be there and witness my own birth. I came out and I wasn't crying so they rushed me out of the room and into the NICU. I rushed to go with and followed the doctor but he shut the door and locked it. This immediately sent up a red flag. My first instinct was to go get Britt but I heard me start to cry in the next room. At first I breathed a sigh of relief but then I heard the doctor say, "Quick switch babies with the one in incubator seven." "Right, doctor." I heard the nurse inside say. Suddenly I heard the doctor and nurse coming toward the door and I ran and hid behind a corner. They emerged pushing an incubator with a very sick looking baby in it. I snuck into the NICU just as the doors were shutting. But there were so many babies that it was impossible to see which one was me. So I rushed back to the delivery room where the doctor and nurse had taken the incubator. There were now two more doctors trying to revive the baby that they switched. I watched in horror as the fastest twenty minutes of my life that I knew went by. But they eventually gave up and pronounced the baby dead. I was disgusted as I noticed the first nurse and doctor smile at each other. After they pronounced her dead Britt took me out in the hallway and I explained what I heard the nurse and doctor say. I broke down crying and it took Britt a while to calm me down. She led me out by the hospital sign where we came up with yet another plan. We would go back in time to the same day as we were in and stay in the NICU until the doctor brought me in. we made sure that we were in the NICU only around the time that I was born. It worked. The doctor brought me in and Britt and I pretended to be caring for a baby in the corner.

They didn't even seem to realize that we were there. They went on with their business and as soon as they left we started towards me two nurses came in and took it down the hall. We carefully followed them and they went in a room and shut the door. They got me to cry a loud healthy sounding cry. They high-fived, and one said, "Now we wait for Dr. Brandon and then we inject her with the serum. Then we wait and see if it works." They high-fived, again and we rushed to get another nurse. We got back to that room not even five minutes after Dr. Brandon came into the room. We stood at the door as he explained to the three nurses what the serum would do. It was then that we burst into the room. The main nurse with us, Jona, told me to get a security guard that was sitting down the hallway. I ran faster then than I ever had to him and to get back to the room. Once back in the room I saw that Jona was holding Dr. Brandon in the corner with a needle at his throat. I was shocked but was kind of glad. The security guard got on his walkie-talkie and called his boss to call the police. I almost laughed out loud when the guard didn't tell Jona to drop the needle. I myself took me back to my family with an officer who explained what had happened and that their child was still alive. They cried tears of joy. It wasn't until hours later that I realized that if that baby was really me then I shouldn't be there. Britt and I stopped him from putting in the serum into that baby so did that mean that that baby wasn't me? I was confused and so was Britt. But thanks to Britt asking a doctor about another baby being injected with the serum. They confirmed that the doctor had indeed admitted to injecting the serum into two babies before today and both had apparently died but came back to life. He then sent those two kids to live in the woods in an abandoned cabin so they can have a private life. What was a shock was the fact that he himself was injected with the serum and that he used the two babies fifty-three years ago. The same time that he was injected with the serum he injected the babies. He was just going to do it to two more because he was lonely and wanted a girl with the curses. The other two were boys, Garret and Todd. They wanted to see if they could reproduce. And they proved that they could because a teenage mother named Tina gave up her twin daughters after naming them Lark and Jackie. So I went to the present day and focused on finding another one like me. I found one and we are now living our dream life. It couldn't have ended any better for us.

EYEBALL KING

"You are a fat, lazy and incompetent son! Where is my dinner?! I'm hungry!" Beth yelled at her only child, a son named Keith. He was busy in the kitchen angrily chopping up watermelon. He was use to her yelling and calling him names. But it was beginning to be too much for him. He had had other plans for his future after going to college to be a social worker. He wanted to help the troubled youth in his town that had issues going on at home. But not even three weeks after graduating his mother had a stroke and he decided to take a year off to help his mother. He had no father. His had left when he was still in his mother's womb and neither Beth or Keith had heard from him since then. She yelled at him again telling him to bring the food to her. "Hey, stupid! Where is my food?" This was the final straw. He decided to end all the hurtful words now. It was time to end all of the insults and harsh statements. He grabbed the knife he was using and crept up behind his mother. As she turned to yell at Keith to bring the food he drove the knife into her right eye. She screamed in agony as he withdrew the knife with the eyeball still attached. He then silenced her screams by slashing her throat. Then he calmly closed the windows and put the eyeballs in a jar in the freezer. He could only hope that the neighbors didn't see what he just did. He then carried his mother's body down into the basement where there was a dirt floor. He was supposed to cover it up with cement years ago on his mother's demands. Thankfully for him he didn't do it so now he dug a hole there and placed her body in it. Then he covered it and poured cement over it. Next he went back up to the living room and cleaned the blood up went to bed like this was a daily event. That night he came up with a plan so that he would forever be known as " The Eyeball King." He would go around killing people until he was finally caught. He would start the very next day. And with that thought he fell into a restful night of sleep. He woke the next day and dressed up to go to out to eat at a local diner. He decided that he would find his next victim there. She was a forty nine year old mother of two three year olds. The twins were called Ben and Brad. Their father, Paul, was an accountant and was away on a business trip. Joy decided to take the twins out to breakfast just so she didn't have to cook. Keith pulled in and sat in his truck and looked through the window trying to decide he would pick next. He took one look at the twins and became jealous that they had a sweet and loving family. He chose them for that reason. He chose them because he was jealous of their normal life. He walked in and pretended to look for a place to sit down. He slowly walked up to Joy and her kids and asked them if he could join them. Joy said yes and gestured at the seat across from her for him to sit down in. they ended up talking about their families and where they were from. He came up with a story that his wife was away visiting a sick grandma and that he didn't have any kids even though he wanted some. He decided to wait until they were out in the parking lot to draw a knife on her. They talked for two hours and by the time came for her to leave the diner was empty. Keith helped Ben clean off his face and carried him out to Joy's car. It was as she was buckling her sons into their car seat that Keith pulled out a knife and pressed it into Joy's back. He then forced her into the car and made her drive to the local teen lookout of the town. He then killed all three of them and pushed the car over into the bushes so that no one would find it for a while. He put all three sets of eyeballs into glass jars and went back home to clean himself up a bit. Afterwards he went to a realtor to sell his mother's house. He figured it would be harder to find him if he moved all over the country. So he put Beth's house up for sale and bought a recreational vehicle with the money. During the three months that this was taking place he killed four other people: Larry and Lark Loon, Tina Tong and Melissa Mooch. And even though they were killed around the same place and the same time Keith didn't get caught. As soon as the house was sold and he had bought the RV he hit the road. So far he had eight pairs of eyes and he was determined to get twenty before he stopped. From Minnesota he decided to head towards Kansas to find his next victims. He had heard that his father was living in Kansas and he was hoping that he would come across him. He wouldn't kill him right away, but instead question him about why he left Beth and him. Then he would kill him. He would make his dad suffer for making him suffer all those years. He would get him back for putting him through all of his bad childhood. But first came the challenge of finding him. Kansas was a big state and he could have moved since Keith had last heard from him. He had to do it though. He had to see if him leaving was his fault or his mother's fault. Beth had always blamed him for it, but she also blamed him for everything that went wrong. So he hit the road and started collecting eyeballs. His first Kansas victim was a horse ranch owner and her husband: Candee and Jerry Jockey. They were old friends of Keith's dad so he chose them. He was hoping to get information from them about his dad. Unfortunately all that he found out was that his dad was still living in Kansas but they were unsure of where he was. So Keith killed them. He collected their eyeballs and put them in the freezer in his RV. He went next to a relative of his father. It was Keith's dad's aunt, Sara Sucker. She was living home alone for the past six years when her husband of forty-seven years died. He was actually the one that helped Keith find Sara. He just looked at Cassidy's death certificate and found out where he died. Keith decided to check in on Sara to see if she had seen his father last. As he pulled his RV up into her driveway he looked at her house. It was a two-story brick house that looked like it was built in the fifties. Keith climbed out and slowly made his way up to her house. She answered the doorbell after a few rings. "May I help you young man?" she asked looking at him. He removed his baseball cap and said, "Yes, madam. I'm looking for Sara Sucker. I was hoping that you had information on my father." She looked at him with wide eyes. She stepped back and ushered him into the house. Sara led him into the living room and told him to make himself comfortable while she got some Kool-Aid. She came back a few minutes later with a tray of juice and cookies. Keith noticed that she was shaking as she set the tray down. She took a deep breath and asked whom his father was. "My mother told me his name was Ted Bunt. That is all that I know about him." "Why don't you ask your mother about him?" Sara asked. Keith was prepared for this question. He told Sara that his mother had just died of a heart attack. She apologized and looked down at the floor. "Well, the last I heard of him he was living in an apartment a few towns over. He never mentioned having a son." "He left my mother when she was pregnant with me. I don't even know whether or not he knows I exist." Keith said. "Ted probably didn't know because he never mentioned Beth after he moved back to Kansas. How about I give you his address and you can drop by and see him." Sara said. Ted smiled and said that that was great and that he would love that. She wrote down his address and bid him farewell. For some odd reason Keith didn't have the urge to kill her like he did with everybody else. He figured that the reason that he didn't want to kill her was because she was older and she had helped him out so much. Sara had actually given him the address to the very person that he was after. Even Keith didn't fully understand why he chose not to kill her. He kind of felt sorry for her. Here he was, a total stranger, coming to her own doorstep and was asking for information of a man he didn't know. But she was very willing to give Ted's address to a man she didn't know. Sara, like Keith, seemed to trust the other person. Keith trusted her and she trusted him. That was all that mattered. As Keith pulled out of her driveway she waved at him through a window and he waved back being glad that he didn't kill her. He slowly made his way to his dad's house to meet him for the first time in his life. He was having a hard time deciding what to say to him. He had no idea what to say to him. Would he just kill him like he wanted to do or question him and then kill him? Suddenly he was already pulling into Ted's neighborhood. He decided to question and then maybe kill him. Because maybe he really didn't know that he existed. Maybe his mother was lying to him all those years when she said that Ted left because he didn't want any kids. He pulled up in front of a large Victorian house thinking that he had the wrong address because there were eight kids in the yard that were fifteen or younger. He double-checked the address on the paper that Sara gave him and then got out of his RV. By then he had gotten the attention of the kids. They were watching him and the youngest ran into the garage where there was a man working on a large, old van. The little boy pointed at Keith as the man turned around and he started to walk to Keith. "Um, hi. My name is Keith Comet. I am looking for Ted Bunt." He held out his hand and Ted shook it saying, "Well, you found him. I'm Ted Bunt. How may I help you?" Keith took a deep breath and said, "I was wondering whether you remember a woman named Beth Comet?" Ted's eyes got wide and he whispered, "Did you say Beth Comet?" Keith nodded. Ted stood in shock and awe." Let's go inside and talk." He finally said. Ted led Keith into the house straight to a small library where there were mostly kids' books. They sat down and Ted went to get a couple beers. He quickly returned and sat down beside Keith. He took a deep breath and asked how Keith knew Beth. He simply replied that she was his mother. Ted inhaled sharply and asked when Keith was born. He told him August of 1989. "She lied to me." Ted whispered. "Excuse me?" "Your mother lied to me when she said that she had a miscarriage. A couple weeks after she told me she was pregnant she told me she had a miscarriage." He said. "Listen, Keith, I am so sorry that you grew up without me. It wasn't fair. Did Beth pass away? Is that how you found me?" he asked. It was Keith's turn to take a deep breath. After thinking for a second he decided to confess to his father what he had done since he was honest to Keith. He broke down and told him what he had done and where everyone was hidden. By the time he had spilled all the beans, he was crying. Ted hugged his son and cried with him until they could cry no more. They then decided to secretly call the police in Minnesota and in the town where the rancher friends of Ted lived to tell them where they all hidden. After they did this Ted introduced Keith to his brothers and sisters. There was his wife, Jesse, and their kids Holly, Jeni, Hannah, Lisa, Lara, Ryan, Garret and Todd. Keith settled down with his new family and lived happily ever after.

FORTUNE TELLER

"What have I done?" Ben asked himself as he looked down at the dead cow that was lying in front of him. He couldn't believe it. The old fortuneteller was right when she said she would curse him and his family if he didn't listen to her advice. But now it was too late. He was cursed and there was no way to change it. He was now and forever a vampire. So were his wife, Joy, and their kids: Brad 2, Tina 11, Lark and her twin sister Melissa 13. They were all part of Beth's curse and it was all Ben's fault. He was supposed to take in Beth's son and raise him as his own son, but he chickened out. He didn't want another kid because he didn't even want to have a baby after Tina was born. Brad was totally an accident. Suddenly the barn door burst and Tina walked in through a pouring rain. "Daddy, what's wrong with that cow?" she asked. Ben jumped up and led her away from the cow saying, "It just died of old age, sweetheart. Now go back inside the house." "But mommy said to come get you for dinner. We are having meatloaf, your favorite." She said with a sweet voice and a bright smile. Ben managed a weak smile and sent his daughter back to her mother. She went reluctantly looking back as she left. Before going back to the house he took the cow's dead body out behind the barn. On arriving at the house he found that the kids were already eating but Joy was standing in the kitchen crying. Ben cautiously approached her and wrapped her in a hug. He asked what was wrong but the kids started arguing and she left to deal with them. Once the kids were fed, bathed and put to bed Joy approached her husband. He figured that she would approach him after the kids were out of the way. "Listen, honey, I think that I know what this is all about and I can explain it. I-" "I'm pregnant." She said cutting into his sentence. He stared at her hoping that she was wrong. This was the last thing that they needed, especially with the curse. Ben looked down for a minute then back up at Joy. Tears were streaming down her cheeks. After staying up most of the night they decided to keep the baby but Ben would go and talk to Beth to lift the family curse. There was a slim chance that she would lift it, but they had to try. Bright and early the next morning he left to go to Beth's farm that was a thirty-minute drive away. Ben blamed himself for the curse because he never consulted Joy on taking in Larry. Beth had walked by with her son in her arms and stopped in front of the Shoe house. Ben figured that the only reason that she wanted this family to take in her infant was because they had a lot of kids and love for them. Ben was working in the field close to the road and Beth motioned for him to come over towards her. She told Ben that if his family took Larry in she would bless him and his family. He turned her away and went back to work ignoring the fact that she said she would curse him for denying her son. He figured that she was just some loony old hag who didn't want to take care of her kid. But that wasn't the case. She wasn't Larry's actual mother, but instead a woman that had found the baby on the side of the road. She only wanted for him to be raised by a loving family. As Ben pulled up in front of her shack he saw her in a rocking chair rocking Larry. She didn't look up at Ben but she said, "So, you have come back. Is it because what I predicted came true? Be patient and your family will change into one too." Ben sat down in the chair beside her and said, "Please, I'm begging you. Remove this curse and I will take in Larry. Just please- please lift this curse." The fortuneteller sat quietly before giving Ben an answer to his plea. "I am sorry for your family, but I cannot lift the curse. It is your punishment for being self centered and conceited. You may go now." She said this last part more matter of fact than a question. All that he could do was get up and go home. As he walked away he heard her chuckling at him. When he arrived back at home he saw the twins were feeding the goats and Tina collecting eggs from the chicken coop. Ben waved at them and walked into the house. He found his wife in the kitchen cleaning up the breakfast dishes. She quickly turned and asked him how it went. He shook his head and sat heavily in a dining chair. Joy immediately started crying again. Ben took her hand and said, "I have an idea. It's a little crazy, but it just might work. What I am thinking is that we sneak over to Beth's house and kill her while she's asleep." Joy looked at him with wide eyes. She sat contemplating the idea, but she nodded and agreed to do it. That night they stayed up again and made plans to kill Beth. They decided to do it that Sunday after they got a few nights good sleep. But by the time that Sunday came the curse had spread from Ben to Joy. She and Ben had both stopped eating and was surviving on cow blood. They could only hope and pray that it wouldn't spread to the kids and that killing Beth would stop the curse. They had Lark and Tina watch the younger kids while they were on their secret mission. They successfully managed to sneak into her house and decapitate Beth. They decided not to kill Larry but instead to finally take him in. They didn't really want to since they had one on the way. But if they didn't he would die. So when their kids woke up the next morning they had a new brother to play with. They oldest three were confused as to where he came from but didn't ask any questions. All that Ben and Joy could do now was wait and hope that the curse would go away. But the very next day Joy caught Lark chewing on a raw lamb leg. She brought this information to Ben's attention. Together they cried and came to a decision that no parent should come to. They decided that no child, whether it be theirs or not, should have to live as a vampire. They decided to kill all of their kids. They even decided to kill Larry just in case Beth had put a curse on him. As they stood over Brad's crib they said goodbye to him as he slept. Then they carefully placed the tip of the wooden stake and drove it in. They did this four more times and then cleaned the blood off of themselves. Then they went to bed after spending some more time praying for their children and for Larry. The next day they spent the whole day trying to figure out what to do with their life. It just seemed like there was no life left without their children. But in the end they decided to keep living and see if the curse would spread to their unborn child. They figured that it would, but they had to have some hope. There had to have hope that there was a light at the end of the tunnel. There arose a problem though. The spirit of Beth came to haunt the Shoe household. The doors would open and shut on their own and stuff would go flying across the room. Plus the voices of their dead kids could be heard. It wasn't the laughter that made them go crazy. It was the fact that they wouldn't get to see them grow up and get married. They wouldn't get grandchildren from them. There was a chance that they weren't going to become grandparents with their next kid. By the time that their next baby was ready to be born they had just found the body of Beth Joanne. She had no family that would have checked in on her so she was left in her shack for five months. Since she had no family or friends the police were the ones that emptied out her shack and found her final will and testament. Ben and Joy were surprised when the cops pulled into their driveway. They were afraid that they were caught even after they had their kid's funeral. They were afraid that they had unburied their bodies and found out how they died. They had had a closed casket funeral to avoid questions. They had just told everyone that they were in a farm equipment accident and that it was too graphic to have an open casket funeral. But it turned out that they had a letter for them from Beth telling them that she had a way for them to get rid of the curse. She had changed her mind the day that Ben had visited her and would remove it when they came back to talk to her again. Instead they went and killed her. But it didn't matter because they had lifted the curse without knowing it. All that she had to do was kill all of their children. If they murdered their kids they would get automatically get more than twice as many back in the next fourteen years. They were pleased at this news even if they didn't want more kids a year previously. Now they were so glad that the curse was lifted that they named their next baby Beth Ann after the fortuneteller. Then came Keith, Hannah, Garret, Todd, Jim, Dani, Candee, Emma, Jackie, Pete, Frank and Lara.

HOROSCOPES

I'm sure that we all have heard about reading the stars and planets to get our horoscopes, but I have a different, more unique way to get my horoscopes for my friends. I never told them how I got them but they were always curious. Unfortunately now things are different so I am willing to let my secret out. It all started almost exactly thirteen months ago. I was out camping with my best friend Lark, her mother Tina and my mother Melissa in the woods near a lake. I remember that it was late at night and that we were telling ghost stories, trying to scare each other. All of a sudden Tina jumped up and pointed at the sky making us all jump a mile because she was in the middle of a good story. We all looked up and saw a bright green light coming closer and closer. At first we thought it was an airplane but the light was getting greener and greener. After we realized it wasn't a plane we didn't even have time to run for the safe cover of the trees. It was over us and we saw a small round door opening in the middle of the bottom of it. Suddenly we were being sucked up into the hole and into what would be the weirdest time of our lives. Once inside we were dropped suddenly onto the floor and jerked to the side as the ship took off again. I was the first one to look up to see where we were. All I saw was an empty metal room. But we were not alone for long a door hidden in one of the walls slid open. The four of us scrambled to our feet walking backwards as we tried to keep away from the strange creature. And boy did it look strange! It was blue not green with pink hair and it was the same height as Lark only he was slightly overweight compared to Lark. He had what we would call a triple chin and several rolls of fat all over his body. He didn't say anything but instead he raised his hand and some unknown force drew me to it. He held me about a foot away from his hand with me being unable to move or scream. We went through the sliding door and into a room with a metal table and several weird looking machines. He laid me on the table and, to my great surprise, took off a mask. Now standing before me was what looked like a regular looking human being. Next he surprised me by speaking to me in plain English. "Hello, my name is Larry. I am not here to harm you. We want to try to improve a skill that you humans attempt to do. We will need to plant an instrument into you. You may choose where to put it or to put it into one of your friends out there. What is your choice?" I looked at him, dumfounded. I didn't want to be a guinea pig but I also didn't want the others hurt. I decided to talk to him and see what this "instrument" was and what it did. I was about to ask him about it but he seemed to be able to read my mind and said, "All it does is help you give you more accurate horoscope readings. It wont hurt you. That is until we learn that you have told someone about this encounter. When we find out that you tell someone we will send one of your friends down to kill you." He paused and then said, "Yes, I will be keeping all of your friends captive to ensure that you will be keeping this a secret. Do we have a deal?" I took a deep breath and then nodded. He smiled, put his mask back on and left the room through another secret sliding door. He returned moments later with six others and introduced them as Pete, Britt, Beth, Paul, Ryan and Cassidy. All of a sudden they were injecting a purple liquid into me. They read my mind again and said, "This is just our urine. It makes a great anesthetic." I shuddered at that comment but said nothing as I succumbed to it. I awoke ten minutes later in a room where Lark, Tina and Melissa were floating in a similar purple liquid as what was injected in me. They entered the room again and explained what was going to happen now. They would release me and if I went two years without telling anyone our secret the others would be safely released. I nodded in agreement. The next thing that I remembered was that I awoke in our campsite with a note in Lark's handwriting saying that they were called away to Africa and would return in two years. This would be believable because they were all doctors who wanted to help starving children. I made my way back to Melissa's truck and drove back to my house. My husband, Frank was slightly surprised at the note but he shrugged it off. We went to work the next day like usual but something that I did different was put in request to be the next writer for the horoscope writer. I got the job three weeks later because there was only one other person who signed up for the job. The other person made her horoscopes up out of thin air so they didn't really make sense to anyone—even an insane person our boss said. So I was immediately was approved for the new position. My first day of work, I awoke with a knot in my stomach and feeling nauseous. I was as nervous as nervous could be. I didn't feel any different now compared to when the instrument was implanted in my butt. But as I sat down at my desk with my new nameplate sitting on my desk, it was weird to see Dani Livestock sitting on a desk looking so professional and proper. It seemed like I was truly destined to do this job. As I waited for my computer to start I saw a note from my boss giving me my itinerary. He told me to start with only a few if I wanted that the old lady, Heather Feather, had left a few old horoscopes for the next issue so it wasn't necessary for me to do a whole days worth of horoscopes. But as soon as I read them I instantly knew that they were totally wrong. I started typing and before I knew it Kady Mady asked me if I wanted to go out to lunch. I turned her down and immediately went back to work. I only remember a little bit of what I wrote for that first day but when I looked back on it recently I saw the Libra sign that I cut out since my birthday is in Libra's dates. One line that sticks out to this day is there will be a rough time in a relationship of mine. It fit me perfectly without me thinking about it as I wrote it. Two days later Frank said that he was leaving me for my sister Cara. It was a horrible timing for me because I was so stressed out with what had happened the previous weekend. But I never cried over it I felt like it but I now realize that there wasn't any time after the encounter that I felt like crying or getting angry that I actually did cry or yell in frustration. The next ten months passed in a blur. I don't really remember very much other than working. I felt lonely and isolated but then in that tenth month I met a man. And boy was he a man!! He was six foot nine, built like a tank and as handsome as handsome could be. My favorite horoscope came from the day that I met Roger and I will always be thankful for it. It seemed that the aliens knew that I needed that love from somebody—anybody. I was desperate and had never been so isolated. I usually had Lark to talk to, but I was starting to blame myself for her absence. It was my idea to go camping. Roger and I seemed to hit it off right off the bat. He was caring and understanding. We went on at least five dates in the first two weeks of our relationship. He himself had just gone through a divorce but he had a couple of twin boys named Adam and Derek. They were nine months old and were adorable. The only problem I had was that if something happened to their father because of me I would feel so guilty. And it seemed like everyone that I got close to lately something happened to him or her. But when he asked me to marry him on our one-year anniversary I actually said yes to him to my own great surprise. One month later Kady's father walked me down the aisle on my way to become Dani Victoria Mattson. My own father had passed away three years ago and Lark's father didn't want to talk to me because he thought that I pushed her to go to Africa. So he didn't walk me down the aisle as we had planned when we had met seventeen years ago. It was on our honeymoon in Jamaica that he noticed a scar on my left butt cheek. I tried to blow it off when he asked me about it, but he wouldn't let the subject rest. I finally gave in and started crying for the fist time in eleven months. As soon as he told me I felt that there was something different about the air around us. Instead of denying it he confessed that he too had had a close encounter with an alien named Larry. He had been implanted with something that was much worse than my "instrument". He was now six times more fertile than any other man in the world. That is why he had had twins forty-four weeks after being abducted. As soon as we were done telling each other our secrets we saw a green light appear and in that green light was Larry's face. "You have broken the rules. You were not to tell anyone and you must now pay the price," Larry said in a whisper that we both heard loud and clear. He then disappeared and we sat in silence for a few minutes. It was Roger who broke the silence when he asked what would happen to me. I told him and he said that he would be a father to twenty-three children by the time that he was forty. He was only twenty-one so he had nineteen more years to go and twenty-one more kids to go. To my great surprise he said that he would help protect me. We decided that the best way to keep me safe was to kill all three of my soon to be attackers—Melissa, Lark and Tina. I sat down at my new husbands house and waited for the first one to arrive. It took only eight hours after we arrived for Melissa to show up. I had fallen asleep on the couch and when I opened my eyes I saw her holding a knife over her head, ready to stab me to death. I screamed and Roger popped out of the closet and shot her twice in the head. Two days later I was in the kitchen making supper for Roger and me and Lark kicked down the door and started shooting at me. Thanks to Roger he had me put a bulletproof vest on in case he missed shooting one of them and got me. I crumpled to the floor praying that Roger would come out of the bathroom in time to help me. I covered my ears as the gunshots echoed in the kitchen. The next thing I knew Roger was pulling me up off of the floor saying that she was dead. He held me in his arms as I cried trying to comfort me. But he only had ten minutes to comfort me. Suddenly Tina came in through the broken down door with a blowtorch gun and said, "Larry said that if you survive this then you are meant to live and to be back to your usual self. If you aren't meant to live then your children will be raised separately in foster homes thinking that you committed suicide after killing the three of us." and then she pulled the trigger. Suddenly Roger's brother Ted appeared out of nowhere and yanked the gun out of her hands. He then started torching her with it. That was the last thing that both Roger and I remember. We then woke up in the hospital surprisingly unhurt. There were no burns at all on us. Tina, Lark and Melissa really were in Africa helping the hungry and sick children. Apparently Roger and I had gone camping and gotten lost. The police chief and fire chief had found us after three days of being absent from work. Unfortunately nineteen years later we had twenty-four more kids: Beth, Britt, Larry, Deb, Ashlee, Missy, Pete, Paul, Ryan, Cassidy, Kevin, Penny, Jody, Kris, Jesse, Kate, Todd, Garrett, Jim, Jason, Megan, Andy, Will, and Jerry. There were three twins and two triplets, all of who were identical to each of their other siblings born with them. We were pleased to have kids even if it was more than what was planned. We had both agreed to name some kids after the aliens that made us like this, even if they didn't lift the curses. To this day I still have my little instrument planted in me by my own choice. I had a great job that paid well and that I loved. I am actually happy that this happened to me though. After all I met a wonderful man and had some great kids. I am more and more thankful each day.

KIDNAPPED

Death. It can be painful or quick. It can come as a surprise or be expected. It changes from person to person as expected. My death was unexpected and painful. I was at my friend's house spending the night that turned out to be my last night sleeping there. My boyfriend and I had broken up a month previous, but he agreed to let me continue to live with him until I had found a new place to live. It took me longer than expected to find a place to rent because a week after Ben and I broke up I lost my job to a younger, more hip person: Tina Turkey. And boy did her name fit her well. She could make turkey noises and she could swell up just like a tom turkey. Although Tina had been after my job as an accountant the timing was horrible. I wanted to go to my mother, Beth Anne Johansson, for money because she had inherited two million from her dad. She also owned her own business that trained in police officers in what mother called the new way. She was only fifty-three but she was a millionaire. But I promised myself years ago that I would never sink that low. I swore when mom kicked me out at the age of seventeen that I would never go back begging for anything- especially her forgiveness. She and I had got into a fight over what I wanted to do after I graduated from high school. She wanted me to go into the same business as she did but I had always wanted to be my own self and become an accountant. She thought that accountants were slackers and only worked during the tax season. No matter what I told her she didn't want to listen. To me she was selfish. To me it seemed that she only wanted to do what she wanted. Since I had other plans she kicked me out. I wandered the streets for two weeks and then I met Ben at school and I moved in with him and his older brother. Their mother had passed away from cancer two years previous to her sons meeting me. Ben was eighteen and his brother, Paul, was twenty-six. They accepted me as a part of their family right away. I think it was because they were so use to it being just them living together and they wanted a female in their house. Ben and I didn't start dating until I graduated. Paul eventually moved out and it was then that Ben and I started dating. It just didn't seem right to date him while Paul was there. But before we started to date Ben and I agreed on a few things. First: we wouldn't get married. Second: we wouldn't have kids. And third: we would always be friends. The night that Ben died I was sleeping in the main bedroom on the second floor. Ben was in the living room sleeping on the sofa. I heard a loud bang that would have woken the dead had we lived next to a cemetery. At first I thought that Ben had rolled over and fell off the couch again. But it was worse- much, much worse. As I turned on the living room light I saw a horrific scene. Ben was lying on the floor in front of the television with a gunshot wound to the head. Suddenly, a masked person grabbed me on the arm. He was wearing all black and was over six feet tall with big broad shoulders. For some reason unknown to me his eyes were familiar to me. They looked friendly but the death grip he had on my arm told me a whole different story. I don't know why but I didn't scream. I felt that if I did he would kill me. Suddenly there was movement on my left side. It turns out that there was another person standing on that side that was also masked and dressed in black. This masked person was almost as tall as the man but it was a female that had shoulder length hair. I remained silent as they gagged me with Ben's dirty gym sock and blindfolded me. They quickly led me out of the house and into a car parked in front of Ben's house. As we left I said a silent prayer for the soul of Benjamin Shoe. I prayed not only for his soul but also for mine in case the kidnappers killed me just like they killed Ben. I prayed that if it were money that they were after that my mother would forgive me fast enough to save my life. The car that we were in turned so many times that it was impossible for me to keep track of where we were when we stopped. They grabbed me by the arm again and dragged at least a hundred feet and then down a flight of steps. They laid me down on a bed and tied my arms and legs to each bedpost. Then they left me lying there. After what seemed like hours and hours, they returned, removed the gag, and took the blindfold off. They handed me a plate with bread and cheese. "You and I are going to have a little talk. My name is Cassidy and this is Dani. There. Now we know each other. You now have five minutes to tell us how to get a hold of your mother. The faster you talk the sooner you can get out of here." Cassidy said. "Y-you can call my mom at 222-2332. Just mention my name and she will send you as much money as you want." Cassidy nodded and stood up. As he headed towards the door Dani said, "Don't you think we should tie her up again?" He looked me over for a moment and then said, "I think now will be a good time to test her behavior. If she is good and doesn't try to escape then we wont have to tie her up again." And with that they turned and left me sitting on the bed in the pitch-black room. I don't know how long I was left there but it seemed like years. I was cold, hungry, scared and nervous all at once. I had only had a slice of bread and a chunk of cheese in what seemed like days. There was no heat in the room and no blanket to curl up into. But above all else I was nervous and scared that mother wouldn't have forgiven me enough to pay them. I kept asking myself all the same questions over and over. Will mother pay them? How much would they want? Will they kill me if she doesn't pay? How will they kill me? I was so scared and yet I knew there was nothing that I could do but wait. As I lay there thinking these thoughts I was slipping in and out of consciousness. Suddenly, I was awakened by a loud bang. It was Cassidy storming into the room and screaming, "Why? Why didn't she pay us? Why isn't she giving in to our demands?" He suddenly grabbed my hair and pulled as hard as he could, ripping out a handful. He stooped over and looked me in the eye and said in a serious tone, " If she doesn't answer to this evidence then we will send her better evidence. Like your body." They then tied me as tight as they could to the bed and left. If I was scared before it was nothing to what I was feeling right then. I had a horrible feeling that I was soon going to be joining Ben. I knew that I would never be able to tell my mother that I was sorry. She would never know that I still loved her. Even after all our fights I still loved her. Paul taught me to forgive her long ago. I just never got around to telling her that. And I now deeply regretted that. As time passed I continued to slip in and out of consciousness. There seemed to be no end to the silence that came after the kidnappers left. It pressed in on me from all the sides. It seemed to go on and on, like a never-ending story. Finally the door opened and Dani came in with Cassidy at her heels. He pulled up the chair beside my bed after untying me. He sighed heavily and said, "She wants more evidence. She doesn't believe it is you that we have tied up in here. So how do we change that?" I tried to say something but my voice was lost in the fear that was swarming inside me. All of a sudden Dani was lying on top of me and as I looked up from under her I saw Cassidy coming at me with a large hunting knife. I screamed but it was pointless. It was over before I knew it. They quickly exited the room and I was left with a missing finger. I curled up on the bed and tried to put pressure on my wound with part of my shirt that I ripped off of the bottom. I cried until I could cry no more. My tears seemed to come from the bottom of my feet all the way to my eyes. Soon I was all cried out and I was passed out from loss of blood. When they returned I was half alive. They wrapped me up in a tarp and drove to another location.

This time it was a log cabin. They didn't even bother to tie me up. They laid me in a corner. I only had enough energy to wiggle enough to get my head out to look at my surroundings. It was a one-room cabin with no walls separating rooms. It was just a big open space. After straining myself to stay awake long enough to look around, I slipped back into unconsciousness. The next thing I knew I was looking down on my body from the ceiling. Then Cassidy came into the cabin and picked up my body. He carried it through the door that Dani was holding open. I followed them to an open hole in the ground back behind the cabin. They placed my body into it and covered it with the dirt beside the hole. I vowed then to get revenge on these two people that had killed me. I went first to my mother's house and talked to her. It took a while to convince that she wasn't dreaming and that I was her daughter's ghost. The first thing that I said to her after she was convinced was how sorry that I had never came back to tell her that I was sorry. I cried as she said that she was sorry too. Together we came up with a plan to get the money back to mom and to get the kidnappers into jail. We went to the cops and after a few days we had them on our side. It took awhile to convince them but in the end they decided to follow my mother and I to the cabin that I was buried behind to dig up my body. The police said that if they had the body they would find and arrest the two people that were responsible for my kidnapping and death and also Ben Shoe's death. As soon as they came across my body they were quite obviously surprised to see it. With the DNA off of my body they were able to find out that the murderers were a couple that were really named Dani and Cassidy Stick. They had mistakenly left a trail behind when they went into hiding after getting the money from my mother. They had caught a flight to Jamaica and left right away. But they couldn't escape from me. Once I led the police to the condo that they were now living in they were arrested and brought back to Minnesota and tried for two accounts of first-degree murder and kidnapping. They were put in jail for life without parole. I decided, as I watched the trial from above in the corner that I would never give them a moments rest until they were dead. Which with Cassidy didn't take very long. He was murdered three weeks after entering jail. It was over something stupid. He got into a fight over who was going to play pool first: him or another jail roommate, Brad Perk. Even though I didn't get to make him suffer, Brad had done that job for me. Cassidy was beat to death by Brad and Larry Pajerky. But he suffered at least. That is all that matters to me. Thankfully Dani lived to be ninety-three. She was never alone after Cassidy died because when Cassidy was alive I would go back and forth between the two of them. But he was soon out of the way thanks to Brad and Larry. One thing that I did make sure that I did was get close to my mother again. I visited her when Dani was sleeping. We were really close by the time that she died at the age of eighty-one. I now wander the earth because I cannot move on. Thankfully I have Ben to share my time with. It turns out that he stayed behind to see that I was okay. We will forever be together carrying on mom's business of training police officers. I decided to do that to make up some of what I messed up with mother all those years ago. Ben and I now help the dead that have been murdered find justice. So if you need help just call mother's business: Beth's Trainers. Ask for Joy or Ben. They will be glad to help.

MOVIE THEATER

The hooded man entered the dark movie theater alone and undetected. He chose a seat behind a teenage couple that was sharing a bag of popcorn. Nobody took any notice to the man but he took notice to everyone around him. The movie started after showing the usual previews. The movie was an exciting drama and the whole audience, including the teenage couple, was engrossed in it. Once the hooded man was sure that the couple in front of him was thoroughly attentive in the movie he reached down into his bag and pulled out two small needles and a tiny bottle of clear liquid. He quickly filled the needles with the liquid and leaned carefully forward so that nobody would notice. Then he suddenly stuck each teenager with a needle. They were dead within seconds. The man checked their pulse and excited the theater with no one seeing him. After the movie was over the audience stood up and began to leave. A friend of the couple was seating in a seat a few rows below them and he hollered at them, thinking that they were sleeping. When they didn't answer he walked up to them and shook the boy, Derek Feather, to try to arouse him. But when his head rolled over and he saw Derek's face he realized that he was dead. His eyes were wide open and he was white as a ghost. Within ten minutes the paramedics were working on the couple, but it was to no avail. The paramedics soon gave up and placed them in a body bag and removed them quickly and as quietly as they could. But that was impossible. A crowd had already formed around the theater and was waiting for the emergency workers to bring them out on the gurneys. The whole crowd went silent when they saw the body bags. Every head bowed in a silent prayer for the two teenagers. Their bodies were transferred to the city morgue where they were immediately given an autopsy. Both were healthy except for a mysterious drug in their system. What it was they were unsure of but they were certain that that was killed both of them. The worst part for their parents was having to come in and identity their sixteen-year-old child's body. Alyssa Hicky 's mother broke down in tears when they pulled back the blanket to show her face. Alyssa was out on her first date with Derek and her mother was already worried. This incident would only increase that for her younger daughter, Barbara. She was eleven and was already asking her mother if she could go out with her friends. Derek was a different story. His mother was a crack addict and father had left when he was an infant. He was different from his mother though. He was a star athlete and on the honor roll at his high school. He wanted to be a doctor when he graduated. But that dream was crushed. His mother was only upset at the fact that he wouldn't be giving her his check from his part time job anymore. She could care less that he was dead. Her only problem now was trying to find money for her addiction. She also refused to pay for her son's funeral because it cost money that she didn't have. Thankfully Alyssa's parents offered to have him buried near Alyssa. They figured that they were killed together that they should remain close even in death. Although their case was never closed they didn't find out who killed Holli and Derek. But two months later and forty miles away the mysterious man struck again. This time he targeted a group of college girls out on a night on the town. There were three of them: Dani Leech, Beth Johan and Tina Tinsel. They were all going to school for nursing and were just a few months away from graduating. Once again he entered the theater hooded and alone. Once again he was undetected. and once again he sat right behind his victims. He was wise enough to wait till a part in the movie where everybody's attention was on the movie. He reached into his pocket and pulled out three needles from his stash and the tiny bottle of clear liquid. He filled each needle full and one by one he injected it into the girl in front of him. Even the last one to be injected didn't notice. As soon as he was sure that they were all dead he silently left the movie theater without detection. Once the movie ended the whole audience left without noticing the three girls. They were only found when a patron came in to collect garbage. He quickly called for help and two coworkers came and tried to resuscitate the three girls but they were beyond help. They had been dead for almost two hours. There wasn't as big of a crowd as there was with Derek and Alyssa, but word quickly spread that the killer had struck again. The autopsy on the girls showed that the same drug that killed the two teenagers, killed Dani, Beth and Tina. But the question was who was the murderer? There were no witnesses that remembered seeing the hooded figure coming or going from either theater. There were no needles found at either sight. And to add to the confusion there seemed to be no connection between the two cases. The police could only wait and see where he would strike next. But they didn't have to wait long. Only two weeks went by when the killer killed again. This time it was in the same town as the first at a theater across town. He chose a man named Luke Lucky who was in his seventy's and was out taking a break from being in the hospital with his wife, Lark. She was dying of leukemia. He decided to see a romance movie since he missed his wife. Although Luke saw the hooded man enter the theater he thought nothing of it because it was winter and it was cold out. The man sat behind Luke and was quiet. Luke returned his focus to the movie not knowing that he soon would be dead. The hooded man didn't wait as long to take out the medicine this time for fear of being confronted by the elderly man. But his worries were soon over. Luke Lucky was dead and the only witness was now gone. He hurried out of the theater alone. After the old man had been removed from the theater he was taken to the same morgue as Alyssa and Derek. He was given an autopsy and was found to have the same drug as the others in his body. The medical examiner was still unable to determine what the drug was. They were thinking that it was a combination of two or three medications. But what they were would remain a mystery for now. Plus they still couldn't find a connection between all of the murders. It was beginning to seem like they were all random. Once again the police were forced to wait and see when and where the man would strike again. But at first it seemed that he was finished with his killing spree. It was another five months before he struck again. This time he killed in another state. That was about the only thing that was different. The rest was identical to the other murders. He sat behind a woman in a dark theater after entering alone and unnoticed. His next victim was a thirty-year-old teacher named Sara Parrot who was out on the town after her husband, Ted Bunt, told her earlier that he wanted a divorce. She had decided to treat herself to dinner and a movie as a gift to herself. She felt like she needed to cheer herself up. But what she didn't know was that her misery was soon to be over. He waited for her to stop crying and then he injected her with the clear medicine. Everybody just thought that she had fallen asleep. Unfortunately nobody would discover her body until the next day. She was stiff as a board and rigor mortis was already in affect. They had to pry her fingers off of the armrest, cracking her fingers as they peeled loose. The autopsy report was different this time. The mystery drug was in her system but she was close to having liver failure. It was only time before she would die and this way was much quicker and painless. Or at least they thought that it was painless. It was hard to tell what kind of death the victims had because they still didn't know what the drug was. But the police now had a break in the case. A psychic named Jeni Jerky had a gift of touching a deceased person's head and being able to see what the last five minutes of the person's life. Since the only person to actually see the killer before they died was Luke Lucky they could only gather the image of the killer from his memory. They found out that the man was white, in his fifties and was about 5"11'. He was wearing black hoody with black jeans. They now knew what he looked like and what he wore. They had Jeni draw a picture of the killer and placed it out on every billboard across the nation. Unfortunately the only people that took any notice to the pictures were the people in the towns where he had killed. The killer noticed this and moved to a state where he knew that nobody would know about his past. He went into a theater across the country and sat down behind a couple named Lisa and Cassidy Shtitter. They were kissing each other and snuggling each other. They caught glimpses of the hooded man with out him noticing. This was the biggest mistake he made, even if it was without him noticing. This was the break that the police needed. The couple died without anyone realizing it and the man exited without notice. Once the police from California and Oregon realized that there was that murder and the murder of Melissa Monkey and her son Keith, they rushed over with the psychic Jeni to see if they saw the hooded man. Melissa and Keith didn't but Cassidy and Lisa did see him. They were lucky enough to see his face and Jeni was able to get a clear picture of his face. He was Caucasian with a bushy gray beard and mustache. He had green eyes and pudgy cheeks. Now the police could put a face to the body that they already had. It was now time to put a new law into affect. You couldn't wear a hooded sweater into any public place. They thought that this would stop the murders, but they were wrong. The man walked into a theater in Florida and put a hooded sweater on in the bathroom. He managed to bring a backpack into the theater because he posed as a student. To add to the problem he had shaved his face. The two men he killed this time were twin brothers named Ryan and Roger Rooster. He killed them the same way as all of the other people. He injected the mystery drug into the back of their neck and they were dead in seconds. He headed out of the theater but before he got to the door of the room he was in he removed the hooded sweater. The new murders confused the cops. They thought for sure that the new law would stop the killer, but it didn't. He was still on the loose and it seemed as if he was unstoppable. The police decided to try video cameras. There weren't many in theaters and it seemed like the killer knew that. All of the theaters that he had killed in had no cameras in them. The police decided to put cameras in every theater without notifying the public in hope of catching the killer. And it worked. The next time that the killer struck he was seen on camera in the bathroom changing into the hooded sweater. They caught him injecting the medicine into Lindsay and Adam Moore. The manhunt was now in full affect. The whole country knew whom to look for and he was caught in a suburb of Chicago attempting to murder Kate Kisser. The man was later identified as Larry Booth, a descendent of John Wilkes Booth. He was charged with all of the murders and put on death row where he is currently awaiting the electric chair.

MURDERED

It was a scene of total destruction. There was blood on the ceiling and the wall. Then there was the streak of blood going from the corner out the door. But whose blood it was we didn't know. There were a lot of things to investigate to find out what had taken place here and why. As I stood in front of the crime scene my partner, Candee Candy, came up behind me and asked, "Listen. We have a lot of stuff to do. We can't stand around doing nothing. I just checked with the landlord of this apartment building and he said that there were two people living here. The first is a man named Adam Apples. The second is his girlfriend, Lindsay Loopy. I'll get in contact with their family and you help by interviewing neighbors. There is also a camera in the elevator so get the film from the landlord. Let's get to work, Justin." She added giving me a playful punch on the shoulder. I sighed, closed my eyes to say a silent prayer and went to work. Seven grueling hours later I was back at the local police station putting together the pieces of evidence that my team had collected. Candee came in and sat down behind her desk looking very tired. She rubbed her eyes and said, "Well, we have good news and bad news from the families. Adam had no family and Lindsay's family don't want anything to do with her because she ran away from them when she was fifteen to be with Adam who was nineteen at the time. So I guess the state will have to pay for their funerals. What did the forensic team find?" I groaned and said, "Well, there was only one type of blood found at the scene and there were chunks of blonde hair ripped from the root found near the door. We think that one of the victims is still alive because there is only one type of blood. But what we can't figure out is why did he take the other body? The perpetrator didn't take jewelry, money or ID's with him. So why take the body? Why not rob the place while he was there?" I sighed and shrugged my shoulders. This was turning out to be a very tough and frustrating case. Suddenly the phone on my desk rang. "Detective Justin Michael Mitchell." I said picking up the phone. A raspy male voice said, "If you want to see Lindsay Loopy alive again then you must send two million dollars to the train station on Friday at three in the morning. You must set it down in the far back car and leave. If there a trace or any police are found near that area she will be killed and I will send her body to you piece by piece. Is that clear to you?" I started to reply but I heard a click as he hung up. I turned to

Candee opened mouth. When I finally found my voice I told her what he had said. We then tried to trace the call to see where it was from but to no avail. The call was too short. We now knew that at least one of the victims were alive. But what about Adam Apples, was he dead? Or was he being kept with Lindsay? If he was then why did they only ask about Lindsay? Did they know that she was the only one that had family? There were too many questions and no answers. As my partner and I talked about it we were called down to the lab to go over the evidence. When we arrived at the lab we went directly to Beth Anne Jam. She was in charge of the lab but was also assigned to our case. As she turned around we saw a look on her face that told us that we were about to receive bad news. "Are you sure that you are prepared for what I am about to tell you?" I heard Candee groan from behind me but I just nodded my head. "Well, to start with the blood on the wall has brain tissue in it. There is only one type of blood and it matches Adam Apples' blood type. The hairs are mostly from the woman, Lindsay Loopy. Considering how much blood that was on the scene the chances that he is still alive is extremely slim." Candee stepped up and asked, "When you said that the hair mostly Lindsay do you mean that some isn't?" Beth nodded and said, "Some are short, brown male hairs." We nodded and she continued on. "We have the video from the elevator. At the time of the crime there were three people entering the elevator. They were hooded and were wearing black. One was definitely a woman. She had short reddish brown hair and was about 5'4". One of the two gentlemen was tall and scrawny. The other was shorter and huskier. He was almost bald but still had some hair, especially coming from his ears and nose." "Do we know if they are somehow connected to the victims?" I asked Beth. She shrugged and said, "You'll have to interview all the residents in that apartment building to know if they are familiar." I nodded and Candee and I left to interview them. Thankfully it was in the evening so most of the people were home. We got nothing from the people in the apartment, but when we left to head back to the precinct a woman came rushing towards us from the alley of the apartment building. She leaned into us and whispered, "Their names are Lara Lucid, Keith Livestock and Larry Snooper. They live in apartment 66B on the sixth floor. But you didn't hear it from me." She then turned and walked back into the alley. My partner and I quickly looked at each other and then hastened to apartment 66B. When we knocked on the door we heard a dog barking. "Saint Cassidy Police Department! Open up!" I yelled. We then heard a lot of banging and yelling. When nobody came to the door we decided to break it down. We were greeted by a friendly pit bull. But as we looked into the living room we saw a man and a woman leaving through the fire escape. Candee grabbed the woman and I grabbed the man. We each had to wrestle the suspects to the ground but we eventually got them handcuffed. Back at the precinct we tried to get information out of them as to where the other suspect was, but mainly where the victims were. Unfortunately they were not giving in. we tried the good cop bad cop theme. Then we tried the tough cop theme. But our efforts were useless. They were not going to budge. So my partner and I decided to go back to their apartment to see if the forensic team had come up with anything. Upon arriving the team was knocking on walls trying to find a secret passage or cupboard. The only room that they hadn't checked was a closet in the office/bedroom. When I asked Beth why they hadn't checked it she merely said that it was too small to hold anything. I volunteered to check it out. She said sure and went back to work. I knocked on the wall on my left first. That one and the one to my right were fine, but when I knocked on the back wall it caved in. there behind it was the body of Adam Apples. He was shot twice in the head and looked as if he had been dead for 48 hours. I hollered for help and when Beth looked in at me she screamed. "Get a forensic expert in here right now!!" Suddenly there were a ton of people in the closet. And let me tell you, if it was small in the beginning it became a lot smaller with everyone in it. They pulled him off of me and I ducked out of the way. Candee gave me a pat on the back and we headed back to the precinct to confront the suspects. They now had a body to connect them to the couple, but where was the other body? The other detectives had not been able to get them to crack. They were relentless in giving up any information. But when I went into the gentleman's interview room it seemed as if he knew what I knew. He sighed and said, "So you found him?" I nodded and sat down in front of him. "I'll tell you what happened if you cut me a deal. Okay?" he said with a strained voice. It seemed as if he was bursting to talk. I figured it was because he knew he was in major trouble. He stretched and then started talking. "We only did it because we were strapped for cash. We figured her family would pay and then we would just let her go. She is being held with Larry Snooper. He was the tall scrawny guy that was in the surveillance video that Officer Randall told me about. I wont tell you the exact location because there are people out there that know me and will come after me when I get out of jail.

But I will tell you it is in an abandoned warehouse." He then laid his head down on the table. I got up and went to check his story with the woman, Lark Lottery. She groaned and cussed when I told her what Keith Livestock had said. "So he was a weakling. He cracked under the pressure. Well guess what? I am not saying anything. She deserves to die. So did Adam and there is nothing you can say or do to change my mind. So get lost." I saw that I was at a dead end so I left. But in a way Lark had confirmed what Keith had told me. I then set up a team to do research to find all warehouses in the county that were abandoned. Next I went to the city morgue to see about Adam's autopsy and if there were any other evidence in his body. The medical examiner was Tina and Brad Thyroid. We had worked on quite a few cases in the past thirteen years that I had been a detective for Cassidy County. Candee and I walked up to the building talking about how Keith had finally cracked because I took the time to check that closet. She was very proud that I took that initiative to do so. We agreed together that we would talk to the whole forensic team and remind them how important it is to do a thorough job. Once we were inside the building we went straight to the back like we usually do. "Hey, you two!" we heard Brad yell at us. He waved us over toward a body covered by a white sheet. He uncovered the head and it was indeed Adam Apples. Even with a hole in his head he was still recognizable from pictures that I had seen of him. "What do we have here with this guy?" Candee asked Tina as she came near us. "Well, we have a 5'11" twenty-nine year old male. He died from a gun shot to the head. He was beaten before he was shot most likely from a struggle. There was dirt and hair under the nails. We ran the DNA from the hair and it was found in the system belonging to a man named Larry Snooper. He was charged with aggravated battery assault seven times spending a total of five years in jail." We remained silent through out this. We now had enough evidence to convict all three suspects. As Candee continued to talk to Tina and Brad I answered my ringing phone. It was Detective Melissa Moocher telling me that they had located the warehouse and were sending several police cars to it. She gave me the address and I grabbed Candee by the arm and dragged her out explaining as we went out towards the car. We went as fast as possible to the warehouse. Thankfully we weren't very far away. We got there in ten minutes before anyone else was there. We approached it slowly without our sirens on. We wanted to use the method of surprise so there weren't any more deaths. Back up was there within five minutes of Candee and my arrival. Once we were all out of our vehicles I motioned for some to go right, some to go left, some to go through the front and the rest to go around back. Five, including Candee, stayed by the vehicles to watch the upper windows. But suddenly a grenade was thrown from an upper window towards the cars. There was nothing anyone could do. It was too late to move. They all died. We then stormed into the warehouse guns drawn and looking for revenge. Once inside we began searching for Lindsay and for Larry. It was probably the most intense fifteen minutes of my life. Thankfully we found Lindsay alive and well. She was a little bit beaten but other than that she was fine. It turns out that Larry wasn't alone. Keith had apparently used his free phone call to call in help. We ended up arresting six others: Derek Dude, Kyle Key, Ryan Rufus, Levi Genes, Ben Shooter and Paul Patter. But what else we found in the warehouse was truly disturbing: eleven bodies. They belonged to Lisa Kipper, Dani Dummy, Frank Fritters, Peter Olsen, Dale Dingy, Jerry Jumper, April Pawe, Garrett Goony, Jim Joke, Doug Hungry and Debbie Cakes. The nine suspects that were arrested were all charged with twelve cases of first-degree murder and are in jail for life. Keith was put in jail for life because he tipped off the other suspects. Next we had the grueling task of finding the families of the victims found in the warehouse. But we got even more bad news when we collected the bodies. The warehouse was a slaughterhouse that belonged to a man named Paul Paulson. When we went to ask him if he knew what was going on in his warehouse. But we walked in to see six women's bodies. They belonged to: Dawn Dusky, Katie Kilt, Kristin Gnome, Jesse Mantel, Kate Marsh and Kris Looker. He was also charged with murder, but unfortunately we couldn't connect him to the other murdered bodies so he was sentenced to fifty years. It was the hardest case and also the saddest case I had ever worked on. I will never forget my partner of thirteen years. I retired after that case because I couldn't stand to see another case like that.

Prisoner

It was suppose to be a simple mission. We were to go to planet Keith and pick up a prisoner. Then return home and have him tried for desertion of the Planet Larry Army. He was fighting in a battle over on planet Katie when he suddenly disappeared. It was common that he had left because of the war that was going on. It had been going on for seven years and hundreds of people and aliens from all over the universe had died so far. Everybody was hoping and praying that the war would be over soon and that all of the death and destruction would be over. All that we knew about our mission was that there had been no contact from anybody on that planet and that we might be facing a hostage situation on that planet. The headquarters left a message saying that the people from planet Katie might be holding everybody from that planet as a hostage. We left as soon as we got the message to get the prisoner. The flight was quick and uneventful. We made it there in record time. But what we saw when we arrived shocked us. There was nobody out on the streets, in the stores or anywhere. We slowly made our way to the local jail where the prisoner was suppose to be. As we approached the jail it also appeared deserted. But as we went inside and rang the bell we heard movement from one of the back rooms. An elderly lady came out of the back door and said, "What do you want?" This took me aback. I didn't even know this lady and she was being rude and inconsiderate towards my crew and me. I stammered a little bit before I said, "We are here to pick up prisoner 5363748 to transport him to planet Larry for a desertion trial." The woman said nothing but turned and went to the back room. She returned ten minutes later and with her was the prisoner. But it didn't look like the prisoner that I knew a few from the pictures in his file. He was supposed to be a dark green with bright pink eyes and perky ears. Instead he was purple with yellow eyes and droopy ears. He looked at me for a few seconds, and then looked down at the floor. "You will need to sign a few papers in order for us to release him into your care," the woman said sliding a stack of papers across the desk. I signed them so quick that it was sloppy, but I didn't care. I was in a hurry to get my crew and the, apparently very sick, prisoner. I had a strange feeling that we were all in extreme danger. As we left the woman at the desk to head back into the back room and the prisoner pulled my shirt. I bent over and he whispered in a loud anxious voice, "Please! We must get out of here! We are all in grave danger! We must leave at once!" "Okay, okay. Would you like me to carry you to our ship?" I asked in a gentle voice. He nodded vigorously. I bent down and picked him up. There was no way he could have weighed more than fifty pounds. He was dangerously underweight for someone of his species. He should have weighed at least ninety pounds. I carried him at almost a full run back to the ship. I took him straight to my cabin and told my crew to take off right away. I wanted to question the prisoner about what was going on at that planet. I told the prisoner to have a seat on my bed and that I would return with a big plate of food. I rushed to the kitchen where the cook, Tina Turnover, had already made a meal for the crew. I quickly explained the problem and she said that she would make other food for the crew. She gave me all of the food on a tray and I carried it back to my cabin. As I set the tray down on my desk the prisoner was staring at the food like he had never seen food before. "Go ahead and eat. We can talk after you finish eating." I said motioning towards the food. He jumped up and started shoveling handfuls of mashed potatoes into his mouth with his hands. "Whoa, whoa! How about we use silverware?" I said trying to laugh. He backed up and looked down at the floor as if he had done something wrong. "It's okay, buddy. You can still eat. Just use a fork and knife." I smiled at him and he almost smiled back. But he didn't. He just went back to eating only at a slower pace. When he had finished eating all of the food I led him back to my bed so I could talk to him. I decided to start off by introducing myself to him. "My name is Beth Jonson. Can you tell me your name?" I asked even though I knew. I wanted to keep the conversation light and friendly. He answered, but it was so quiet that I asked him to repeat it. "Cassidy." "Well it's nice to meet you, Cassidy. Did you enjoy your meal?" he nodded and I decided that it was time to start interrogating him about planet Keith. "So, Cassidy, can you tell me about what was going on at that town? Do you remember what happened to you after the battle on planet Katie?" He slowly nodded. "Can you tell me about it?" Cassidy took a deep breath and started talking. "It all started five weeks ago. I was wounded at the battle and I was taken away to planet Keith to get better. But when I got there the unthinkable was already in effect." He paused there and I asked him what he meant by that comment. He continued in a slightly quieter voice. "The infection was already starting to spread. People were already passing it on. It wasn't their fault. Nobody had ever had this infection before. There isn't even a name for it as far as I knew. I don't think that anybody knows what it is." "Can you tell me what the symptoms are?" I asked. "Well, first you don't have any appetite. Then you want raw meat. And then-" he stopped and looked at me. He took a deep breath and continued on in a shaky voice. "Then you drink blood." He then broke down and started crying. I then picked Cassidy up and placed him on my lap I held him until he was done crying. I asked him why he was crying and he said that he was going to make a shocking confession. "It was me," he said. "What about you?" I asked. "I have the virus," he whispered. I stared at him for a moment and then asked him, " Do you think that you might be mistaken? Did you actually get bitten?" he shook his head no. I then breathed a huge sigh of relief. "Well, let's not jump to conclusions. Let's just wait and see if you start showing the symptoms and if you don't then we will just take it from there. Does that sound good to you?" He nodded and then looked up with a small smile on his face. I returned the smile and said, "How would you like to meet my crew?" I asked. Cassidy nodded and we left my cabin and headed towards the engine room. Upon entering I saw that most of the crew was already relaxing. "Listen up, people." I hollered. "This is Cassidy. He is going to be bunking with me until we land." The crew said hello and then went back to talking among themselves. I took Cassidy by the hand and led him to each crewmember. First I introduced him to the main pilot, Derek Donkey, and the copilot Lark Leno. Then I introduced him to the other members. Thankfully there was a small crew because Cassidy seemed to be getting more and more confused as I introduced him to each member. After meeting the other three crewmembers in the engine room. There was Paul Iceberg, Pete Oakland, and Melissa Monkey. The other four members, Kyle Keeper, Maren and AJ Spencer and Missy Whitmore were in their cabin after having Cassidy meet them we headed back to my room. He asked if he could take a nap and I said that we both should probably turn in early. He fell asleep right away but I lay awake for a long time thinking about what he had said. I finally fell asleep hoping that he would be fine and that he wouldn't be charged with desertion. I decided to go on the witness stand and testify for him. I would tell the court system that he didn't actually desert the army. When I awoke in the morning Cassidy was setting on the end of my bed staring at me with his eyes wide open. I sat up right away and asked him what he was doing. He shrugged and asked me what was for breakfast. I chuckled and told him that we would go get something to eat after we both had had a shower. His eyes went even wider but he nodded and followed me to the separate shower stalls. After we were done showering we went to the kitchen and I introduced him to Tina. Once again he ate in a hurry but at least he used his silverware this time. He had four helpings until he sat back and sighed, rubbing his stomach. I laughed and asked him, "Are you full, little guy?" he nodded and smiled a big smile at me for the very first time. Over the next few days Cassidy wandered around the ship talking and playing games with the crew. But on the fifth day Maren was turning pale and wasn't eating as much. Unfortunately I didn't noticed this and it spread to AJ next. I guess it was because they were a married couple. A week after we picked up Cassidy Tina came to me saying that there was missing meat. I knew that someone was infected but the question was who? Was it Cassidy? It didn't seem likely because he was still eating a lot of food and he wasn't as purple and he was now joking around and talking to all of the crewmembers. So who could it be? I decided to wait and see if someone stopped eating and sneaked raw meat. But soon the meat was no longer being stolen. It seemed that the infection was gone and I breathed a sigh of relief. But I breathed too soon. The infection had not gone away. It was only beginning. Two days before we were to return to planet Larry it all went wrong. Tina noticed something and she brought it to my attention right away. She noticed that meat was missing once again. There was over thirty pounds of meat missing in the past two days. We met in my bunkroom while everybody was in the engine room talking and playing around. We got to talking and we soon decided that the best and only solution would be to kill everyone with the infection. After we killed them we would land on the nearest planet, which would be planet Brad. We agreed that it would be best if we killed them at night instead of during the day so they couldn't fight back. Tina did some research and found out that in order to kill some one with this virus you had to drive a wooden stake through the person's heart. We first went to Maren and AJs room first. It was a hard job that didn't get any easier no matter how many people we drove the stake through their heart. We stood over each person and said a prayer for his or her soul. Tina and I took turns with the stake until all the crew was dead. It seemed like it would never end. But Tina and I got through it. We then headed to the engine room where we realized that there was a huge ice storm going on outside. This meant that we had no radio contact to the outside world. We were forced to land on planet Brad without help. It was a difficult job and one that I regret. I blame myself for the death of Tina Turnover. Of all of the planets to land on why one that was infested with werewolves??

Radio

A radio is what changed my life—and not for the better. The day started out just like any other day, but when I was starting work it took a turn for the worse. Let me back up and explain it all from the beginning. I have worked for a lady named Lark Gold for two years and she is an amazing boss. She is smart, pretty, caring and understanding. She is the kind of person that you treasure as a friend. Her boss is the opposite though. Tina Louise was always barking orders and being rude. She didn't like to let us take breaks. But since she was always smoking on the other side of the building, Lark let us take breaks every half hour but only on the opposite side as Tina's side and only if we were silent so she wouldn't hear us. Tina was also against listening to the radio. She only allowed it because we were quieter with it on. She didn't like us joking and kidding around and she defiantly didn't like us when we were noisy. The day of the radio incident I went to plug in the radio because Tina was out sick with the flu and Lark said that I could plug it in. All of a sudden it electrocuted me across the room into the brick wall opposite of the plug-in by the radio. I crashed through the three layers of brick and landed outside by the picnic table. I don't recall what happened to me between landing outside and waking up in the hospital four days later. From what I was told by the doctors, friends, and family they had shocked me twice but I didn't come back. But when they were in the elevator with me on a gurney taking me to the morgue, I sat up and looked around. The nurse that was in the elevator then fainted from the shock of me coming back to life. Apparently I had been "gone" for seven hours. They say that when you die you see a bright light or tunnels or something, but I didn't. I don't recall any of that happening to me. It was like I was asleep for seven hours and woke up from a nap. The nurse took me back to the emergency room where they ran test after test on me trying to figure out how I had come back from the dead. After they were done with the tests and the results had come back they came in where my dad and mom were sitting with me. They looked puzzled and confused. There were six doctors all together and the one in front sighed and said, "Well, Beth, as you know we ran several tests on you and we can't seem to figure out how you were dead for seven hours and came to again." I stared at him unable to believe what he said. This was suppose to be the best hospital in the state and the doctors couldn't find anything wrong with me? I sat there trying to find a way to ask how they didn't find anything when my dad asked, "So what you are saying is that she is okay and can come home?" The group of doctors looked at each other nervously. Another doctor stepped forward and said, "Well . . . . not exactly. There is something we found going on in her brain that we couldn't figure out." He paused and yet another doctor came forward. "There is a part of her brain that is now active. During previous research on other patients we found that the part of the brain that is in her brain that became active is a part of the brain that only is active in geniuses." My parents exchanged weird looks. "So what you're saying is that I'm a genius?" I asked slowly. "We don't know yet. We want you to stay for a while so we can do more tests." The first doctor said. I groaned and sat back in the bed. The last thing that I wanted was to stay in the hospital. I was frightened and felt even more alone when my parents left. My mother, Dani, worked the graveyard shift at a local hotel as a clerk and she was due to work that night. My dad, Larry, had to be at work the early the next morning so he was also forced to leave. I tried for hours to fall asleep that night but was unsuccessful. When the nurse came in to check my vitals at two a.m. I was wide-awake. She introduced herself as Nurse Deb. Her solution to helping me fall asleep was to give me a big book to read and have me fall asleep that way. After taking my vitals she left and returned with a classic book titled "20,000 Leagues Under The Sea". Soon I was totally absorbed in the book. I lost all track of time until I finished the book and Nurse Deb came in at four a.m. to retake my vitals. I had my eyes closed thinking of the book ending when I heard her enter my room. I guess she had tried sneaking in but since I was awake it obviously didn't work. When I looked up at her she got wide eyed and asked why I wasn't reading the book. I then simply told her that I had finished reading it. She scoffed and asked again why I wasn't reading the book. I smiled and told her to ask me any question about the book. She gave me a strange look and pulled up a chair to my bed. She started out with an easy question. After answering that question correct she asked me a harder question. I continued to answer the questions correctly until she was making me direct quotes from the book. It didn't take long before she was using the book to try and come up with a question to try and stump me. But by five o' clock she gave up and went and got the first doctor that saw mw the night before. Shortly after they left my mother showed up. She had managed to get off work early to come see me. Thankfully she had brought breakfast for the two of us. As we got started eating Doctor Keith Livestock and Nurse Deb came in. I smiled at the nurse and continued to eat my breakfast burrito. Mom looked up puzzled. She asked them why they were coming to take me to get my tests done so early. Doctor Livestock sighed and began to explain what had happened. Nurse Deb was giving me that strange look again. After the doctor had explained everything to me mother looked at me and said in a voice that was barely above a whisper, "But she has never read that book before. She can barely read at a high school level." Both the doctor and the nurse looked as if they were about to faint. After a bit of stammering Doctor Livestock said, "Are you sure? Can you prove it?" mom nodded and went home to get the evidence that they wanted. She returned an hour later with recent report cards and tests stating just what they wanted. After seeing this they said that it confirmed the fact that the part of the brain that only geniuses use I was now using. Over the next three weeks I made frequent visits to the hospital and underwent several tests. At first they were medical tests, then they went to IQ tests. By the time that they were done treating me like a guinea pig I had realized that I was also given a special power that allowed me to see into the future. I wanted to share this with the doctors, but I didn't because I was sick of going through all of those tests. I figured I'd read up on it and learn how to control it by myself. If only I knew better. The only person that I shared this with was Joy Roach, my only friend. She decided that I could test this new power out on her. So we waited until my parents were both out of the house. The two times that had made realize my power was when I was holding hands with my mom and I was an image flash in front of my eyes. I let go before I could see the whole thing. The second time I was getting an IQ test done and I purposely brushed my hand over her and had images pass in front of my eyes. It was after that second time that I realized that I needed to investigate this more closely. So we waited until the coast was clear and then we went into my bedroom, stood in the middle and held hands. As the images passed before my eyes I saw Joy walking down a street that I recognized as my street. Suddenly a car hit her from behind and then took off. I also recognized the car as belonging to Britt Hippo. She was part of the only gang in our town that liked to do mean things to anyone that they could get their hands on. She was the leader of the whole gang—not that there was a lot of people in the gang. It was only she and Kady Cookie, Derek Monkey, Ashley Ashes, Ben Shoemaker, Paul Duncan, Adam Reamer and Adam's wife Cara. They were all well known around town and not even the police could completely contain them and keep them in order. As soon as I saw her being struck by the car I let go very quickly. She gave me a puzzled look and asked what I saw. I stammered a bit, took a deep breath, and told her. She laughed and told me to brush up on my psychic skills. After she started to laugh I started to laugh also. I figured that she was right when she said I needed to brush up on psychic skills. We watched TV for a while and then her mother called and asked her to come home. She gave me a hug goodbye and started walking home. If only we had taken my vision more seriously I wouldn't have let her go home. I would have called the police and told them that Britt was driving drunk. Or something like that so that they would have taken he off the road. I would have given anything to be able to bring her back to my house. But unfortunately she died on impact. When the police came to my house to question me about the accident I decided to tell them that Britt was after Joy just so that they would make the proper arrest in this murder. I had a restless night of sleep that night. I had horrible nightmares about Joy in which I was actually the one driving the car that killed her. Finally in the middle of the night after waking up in a cold sweat for the fourth time I decided to blame it on coincidence. I would try it again the next day on one of my teachers at school. If the same thing happened then I would talk to my parents about my newfound power. The next day was the first day back to school for me. As I was walking to school I decided to test my psychic power on my chemistry teacher Adam Lingo. I had to go talk to him about a big test that I had missed. All of my other teachers had excused me from the work that I had missed but Mr. Lingo was being difficult. He didn't seem to understand that there was nothing that I could do to help being sick. He was a lot like Tina. They were both strict and not very understanding to other people's needs. That is why I would target him and Tina first if the next time that I used my psychic powers that person would die. I got to school earlier than I usually did so I had plenty of time to do my business. I knocked on Mr. Lingo's office door and he yelled, "What do you want?" I stammered a bit and then said, "It's Beth. I'm here to talk to you about my work that I've missed while I was sick." The door opened and I cautiously entered. I already had a plan in my head as to what I was going to do. I held out my hand and waited for him to shake it. He gave me a puzzled look but then took it. I gripped it firmly and closed my eyes for a second. There I saw Mr. Lingo talking to the custodian, Brad, and all of a sudden a girl named Hannah Lock came up from behind and shot Mr. Lingo in the face. I let go and acted as if everything was cool. After I was finished talking to Mr. Lingo I went to gym class. The day seemed to drag on. All of my classes were too easy now and I was anxious to see if the image that I saw would come true. I walked home slowly that day being almost convinced that Joy's death had been coincidental. But after dinner that night my mom was watching the news while I did the dishes and she suddenly screamed my name. I went rushing to her and upon arriving at her side she was staring wide eyed at the TV. I looked and there was a picture of Adam Lingo with a picture of Hannah next to it. Apparently my vision had come true. I stared at the TV so hard I didn't even hear my mother ask if I knew anything about his death. She grabbed my shoulders and made me turn to face her. She shook me a bit and then repeated her question. I took a deep breath and started explaining what had happened over the past two days. After I had finished she sat there was a shocked look on her face. The next thing that I knew I was in the back of my mom's car on the way back to the hospital. I once again underwent a long process of tests and questions. Finally they decided to have me sent to the local asylum. I guess they figured I was dangerous because I was put in a padded room with a heavy door that was bolted shut. The next day they decided to see if I was telling the truth by having me hold a nurse's hand. Her name was Erin Waver. She had been a registered nurse for the past thirty-five years. I was reluctant to do it because I knew it meant me staying in the padded room for the rest of my life. But they forced me to. That was the last time I ever had human contact for longer than a few seconds. That nurse passed away when another patient stabbed multiple times in the face with a scalpel. It has been seventeen years since I last saw the outside world.

Seventeen years away from the fresh breeze and bright sunshine. I guess it is for the best but I do wish I had kept my secret to myself. The only thing that I have to look forward to is monthly visits from my family. Dad and mom, who I know call by their names, have had three more children since I left: Jeni, Lara, and Kevin. I know they are my siblings but I don't feel like they are my siblings. They are more like cousins to me. The only advice I have for anybody is this: Don't take life for granted. Cherish each and every moment of it. You never do think that something as simple as a radio would change your life but anything is possible. Remember that.

Hypnotist

Thunder rumbled in the sky and lightning flashed. It seemed that God knew what I had done. But it was for my mother's best interest. She was the one who wanted me to get married and have children. Although maybe I had taken it too far I thought as I talked to the hypnotist. Maybe tricking a guy to marry me was taking it too far. But mother did have cancer so I figured it had to be done. As we peered into a magical mirror that the hypnotist, Tina Ghost, had she showed me three men that were my choices of available men. First there was Paul Prater. He was forty-five and a divorcee with a daughter named Maren. Then there was Roger Rope. He was nineteen and going to college to be a doctor. Finally there was Brad Branson. He was thirty-seven and was a famous writer for a magazine that was published worldwide. It was slim pickings but I finally decided to pick Roger because he was smart and would make a lot of money in the future. Tina and I decided to nab him at the hardware store the next day. I woke up bright and early the next day and dressed in sexiest dress that I owned. I met Tina at the entrance to the hardware store and we waited for Roger to come out. Tina spotted him first and immediately put him in her trance. Thankfully nobody saw us leading him to Tina's van. As I drove to the secret location that we had picked out ahead of time I then got into the back of the van. Roger was just staring straight ahead and kind of drooling because he was so deep in Tina's trance. It only took five minutes for Roger to "fall in love" with me. I think that maybe we put the spell on a little too strong because two days later we were in the local town church getting married. My mother, Lark, was so proud that she was going to have a son-in-law that she couldn't stop crying. We went on a honeymoon to Cancun paid for by my mother and five months later I received a telephone call from Tina saying we were to be expecting quadruplets. I begged her to change her spell that she had put on me and make it just twins but she refused and hung up on me. I realized six months later that I might have made her angry because I had SIX kids. There were three boys and three girls named Alyssa, Derek, Adam, Britt, Kady and Larry. I went to Tina's house to talk to her about the number of kids I had. Unfortunately she had apparently moved because the house was deserted. I broke down crying when I checked the mailbox and found a letter addressed to me.

I read the letter crying harder and harder. It turns out that she was mad at me because she thought that I was being disrespectful towards her. She finished off by saying that as soon I finished reading the letter the spell on Roger would be broken. The very second that I read that sentence I felt a chill go through my body. I quickly rushed home and was anxious to talk to Roger. He was sitting in the living room looking around very confused. I sat him down and explained what I did to him. Once I was done he didn't yell like I thought that he would. Instead he went directly upstairs and packed his clothes. He was gone by the next day and I was stuck with six kids to raise. I decided to calmly mother to tell her what I had done. She was the one who yelled at me. But she decided to hook me up with Keith Kow. She thought that Dani Kow sounded like a sophisticated name. Even though I didn't think so I was desperate for help raising my kids and he was willing to raise them. He was apparently devastated when I married Roger. We only went on seven dates but it seemed like we were dating forever. We were married a month later when the kids were exactly six weeks old. We didn't go on a honeymoon since we couldn't find someone to baby-sit the kids. It all seemed too good to be true. Three months later I found out that Keith knew about Tina's spell on Roger. He knew because he was Tina's brother. Tina, Keith and their mother Melissa were all hypnotists. He was as angry with Tina as I was because she had hurt me. He cared for me so much that he was willing to help me get revenge on Tina- even if it meant killing her. We turned to their mother who, besides being a hypnotist, was also a psychic. We talked to Melissa and she decided to help. She came over for dinner and after the children were in bed we went to work. We gazed into her crystal ball and it told us that she was in Duluth, Minnesota. We carefully planned out what we were going to do step by step. We decided that the best thing to do was to kill her and hide her body where nobody would find it. We decided to find help with some friends of Keith. There was Luke Walker, Ryan Mat, Cassidy Bass and Beth Baker. They all had experience with this kind of stuff so we were confident in them. We left the babies at a friend's house and left Kansas for Minnesota. Our plan worked out perfectly. Beth went to talk to Tina pretending to want to seduce a man. Once again Tina caught a guy off guard outside of a store and led him to a secret location. It was then that we sprang into action. We yanked open the door and pulled our guns out. We pulled her out of the vehicle and tied her to a big spruce. Surprisingly she didn't yell or fight at all. She merely said that we would regret what we were going to regret what we were doing. The whole time she was chuckling. Once she was tied to the tree we stepped back to try playing a mind game with her. We started joking around asking each other who was going to shoot her and where. Instead of being afraid we realized that she was mumbling under her breath. We told her to speak up. She just grinned and kept mumbling. Suddenly we noticed that there was a smoke appearing around us. It began to choke us. It was Cassidy that noticed that there were shapes in the smoke, which were quickly turning into the shape of a person. Out of nowhere Luke was screaming and grabbing his face. We all jerked around to look at him and what we saw was straight out of a horror story. His skin was literally falling off of his face, like wax on a candle. Ryan and Beth were soon running away towards the van. Unfortunately the man that Tina and Beth were putting a spell on was now watching in horror as we all started to melt. Soon the six of us were just a puddle on the forest floor. The man, Jason, slowly and shakily got out of the van and made his way to Tina. She tried to tell him to untie her but he instead grabbed the closest gun. He pointed at Tina, but was too afraid to pull the trigger. Instead he grabbed the keys from the ground by Beth's puddle. He drove to the sheriff's office and brought the very confused sheriff back to the spot where it all happened. Thankfully Tina was still tied to the tree, but not for long. Just as they pulled up and got out she managed to untie herself. She started to run and when she didn't stop when the sheriff ordered she was shot in the leg. Instead of stopping her she simply blew on it and it healed instantly. After pausing for a few seconds from shock the sheriff emptied his gun into her. Thankfully that stopped her for good. The sheriff then called his back up and waited for them to arrive. The whole time I was watching from above trying to talk to them. Finally as they pulled up and I managed to holler out. I told the eight deputies, the sheriff and Jason that I wanted my brother and sister in law to raise my kids that lived back in Colby, Kansas. They nodded and agreed to pass on the message. To this day I don't regret having my kids. I only regret the fact that I wanted revenge. Thankfully I can still talk to my children and I tell them that revenge is not the way to go. Nothing is worth that risk I say every day to them. I can only hope and pray that they listen. Conclusion:

My final piece of advice to you is to never think you know what is going to happen next. Things rarely end the way that you think they are going to end.

About the author:

My name is Angela A. Taylor, I am a twenty two year old aspiring writer who received a brain injury when I was fifteen. I was hit on the head and was told by doctors a while later that I would never graduate from high school. I would love for them to see me now just to show them how far I have come. Nobody thought that I would do very much with my life, but my life is going exactly the way it is supposed to. I live in the beautiful city of Duluth by Lake Superior. I now have three jobs and I am almost ready to live on my own outside of my group home where I currently reside.